Moving

by

Margaret Nash

Illustrated by
Lesley Hallas

First published
September 05 in Great Britain by

Educational Printing Services Limited
Albion Mill, Water Street, Great Harwood, Blackburn BB6 7QR
Telephone: (01254) 882080   Fax: (01254) 882010
E-mail: enquiries@eprint.co.uk   Website: www.eprint.co.uk

© **Margaret Nash**

The moral right of the author has been asserted in accordance with the
Copyright, Designs and Patents Act 1988

ISBN 1-904904-42-4

Author's Notes

This story is set in a northern city towards the end of the 1950's. It is loosely based on Liverpool, though characters and street names are fictitious.

The 1950's brought a time of great change. The Second World War was over, but re-building was still being undertaken in many areas such as Liverpool and other big cities, and with it came new designs in architecture.

Apart from these changes, attitudes and fashions changed too. Women began to be paid an equal salary to men in many areas of work. More mothers worked, if only part time, but a lot of housewives still stayed at home. Homes were beginning to have more luxuries such as televisions, automatic washing machines and kitchen units, designed especially for kitchen equipment, in place of the old fashioned cupboards. The public still travelled around on public transport generally, so the roads were much quieter with fewer cars. Many streets still had their corner shop and in the north there were placards advertising everything from soap powder to drinking chocolate.

Fashions were becoming more important to young people although the 'teenage market' as such was not yet established. Dance halls were well attended and with the exception of local dances, ballroom dancing was the main form of dancing, often to live orchestras. The Beatles were on the scene in the pop world, although nobody could have foreseen how their following would have grown in the 1960's.

These changes brought freedom to many, but also tensions with the changes and altering values which would become established and sweep into the sixties.

Chapters

1	Don't Tell Dad	1
2	Mum Will Kill You	7
3	Barbara's Boyfriend	14
4	Juke Box Jury	21
5	Fireworks	29
6	Trouble in the Fog	36
7	Enough of Barbara	41
8	The Scare of Our Lives	46
9	Rescue	51
10	Moving On	58

Chapter 1

Don't Tell Dad

"Quick, the bus is coming."

Someone's school beret had landed on top of the bus stop. Amidst screams of laughter the girl shinned up the post and retrieved it as the bus drew into the kerb.

We jumped on board, and shot upstairs, our schoolbags buffeting around, then squashed ourselves three on a seat. I loved the fun we had going into town, but once there it stopped. I was the only girl in our gang who changed onto the number seventy two bus.

"Bye," they chanted as I veered off in front of the town hall to where my bus stood waiting.

I went upstairs and sat down heavily on the back seat. My sister, three years older than me, and in the fourth form, was supposed to catch the same bus, so we arrived home together. Mum liked it that way because she worked in the afternoons at the paper shop. But lately Ba kept missing the bus, or so she said. I was beginning to believe there was another reason. The bus swayed as someone got on. I peered down the stairs but it wasn't her. And then we were off up the Dallow Road. I looked for my favourite advertisements on hoardings, as the bus ground throatily up the hill past the large black buildings with dirty glass windows. Many had spider web cracks in the corners which radiated across the whole windows. They looked derelict but Dad said some weren't – not like St. Luke's Church which was bombed out in the war and still just a shell. Gran had said it would always be a shell, a reminder of the dreadful bombing of Liverpool in World War 2.

We were passing the Regent Street wash house now, and the longest rows of black, back to back houses I'd ever seen, the Wellans. I knew the names of all the streets. First Wellan Street, then Wellan Terrace, then Wellan Avenue and Wellan Place. They all looked the same, with a lav in the corner of the back gardens by the gate posts. Our lav was a shed now as Mum and Dad had made a bathroom up in the attic, but I could remember the smell of the limed lavatory walls from when I'd stayed with Gran sometimes. I remembered the feel of the damp toilet paper hanging on a wire on the whitened wall. Ugh! They were grim places. I remembered going down the steps on a dark cold evening, and the moths fluttering round my torch. Horrid really, and yet the memory didn't seem bad. Grandma always left the door open so the light flooded down the steps and across the yard for me. And she always made a fuss of me when I got back.

"Come and sit by the fire lovey," she'd say. "Don't want you catching your death . . ."

". . . of cold," I'd add, and she'd hug me.

Everyone liked Gran Baker, but I think Ba missed her the most. Gran would let Ba stay up late and they played hairdressers. Gran would put Ba's long dark hair in rags which made beautiful ringlets. Mum hadn't a lot of time for fussing and still hasn't. Gran's death a year ago had upset us all. We were still getting over it but it had hit my sister particularly hard.

"One at a time please."

It was the conductor. We were at Grange Street and the local school mob were clumping up the stairs. The chill of late Autumn drifted off them onto me as they passed. I wondered if my friend Beryl from the Catholic school would be among them but she wasn't.

"Greetings Grammar School Grub." It was Tony Bullock. He'd been horrid to me at the junior school and worse since I'd passed the eleven plus exam, and he hadn't. He stuck out his leg and kicked my schoolbag under the seat in front.

"Fluent in French yet are you?"

"Oh shove off."

I hooked my foot round the strap and pulled the bag back away from the cigarette butts on the dirty floor. Before he got off he dropped a rolled up bit of paper in my lap.

"Bit of news for ye," he said and clattered down the stairs. I unfolded the paper. "My brother's going out with your sexy sister. Says she's real hot stuff!"

I screwed up the paper and kept it in my fist where it burned like a hot potato. Surely not! Not Trevor bull-headed, bragging Bullock. He was horrible, he had thick greasy hair and thought he was the cat's whiskers. He was what Gran would have called a smart Alec. I nearly missed my stop thinking about it.

As I turned into our back street I stopped. There was my sister. She was riding on the back of Trevor Bullock's scooter, her arms clasped tightly round him and her head leaning on his shoulder. Her skirt was rolled up to look shorter. The scooter stopped. She got off and shuffled down her skirt. What was she playing at? I walked on as I couldn't think what else to do. I heard a firework explode in the sky followed by the revving of his motor bike as it shot off again, then Ba's footsteps running up to join me.

"Don't tell Dad," she said. She plucked at my sleeve, "Will you?"

I stopped and faced her. "You're mad," I said, "fancying that dumb cluck. Is that why you keep saying you've missed the bus?"

Her cheeks flushed pink. "Not always," she said. "I'll come home with you on the bus tomorrow, promise. Cross my heart Ann. But don't tell. You know it will only upset Dad." She knew I wouldn't want that. Our dad was not a strong person, Mum said. He'd been shot down in the war all those years ago, and it had made him quiet, apart from when he had one of his turns. He wasn't keen on going out much so Mum often went out with her sister. As we walked down the path we could hear him playing the piano quietly to himself. That's what he did a lot of, played and lost himself in the music.

"O.K." I said. "I'll not tell."

Chapter 2

Mum Will Kill You

We began getting tea ready. It was what we always did, because Dad gave piano lessons at this time whilst Mum worked in the paper shop. I glanced down at the patches of red polish on Barbara's nails as she stood by the sink picking them.

"They're so strict at that school you can't do a bloomin' thing. Old Crag Face saw it in the maths lesson and told me to take it off." I laughed. Miss Crag missed nothing. We all knew that. "I could leave school if I wanted to," she added.

I stared at her. "Leave? What, now?"

She nodded.

"Don't be stupid. You've to stay at the Grammar school until you're sixteen."

"Haven't."

"Have."

"Trev says if you pay ten pounds you can get off once you're fifteen. They can't keep you there. He's installing juke boxes in cafés."

"Well he didn't go to a Grammar school. You're good at things. You'll pass all your exams. Anyway I thought you wanted to do music and be a singer."

"Yeah well, it's all got boring."

I knew she'd dropped out of the school choir a few weeks ago, and stopped singing in the choir at church.

Mick, from next door, was coming up the steps for his piano lesson. I opened the door for him.

"Give this to your Mum," he said, holding out his mother's Littlewood's shopping club catalogue.

"Glory be!" I sagged under its weight.

"We've just got a new telly on Hire Purchase from it. Mum says it will be paid for in a couple of years."

"Lucky you. No chance of that here," chimed in Barbara.

"Can I come round and watch Juke Box Jury tomorrow then?" I asked as I put the catalogue down on the formica table.

"Yes if you like. It's on at six."

He went into the front room and was soon playing scales for Dad.

"He's one of Dad's best pupils," said Barbara.

"Like you are, or were," I said. "I used to listen to you and Dad playing duets last year lying on my bed." I wished I was like her - good at school, good at singing too. She'd done solos in the Church choir, and once sang at the Cathedral at a special service. I lifted the slab of potted meat from the pantry, opened a tin of mandarin oranges and trickled some milk into Smokey's dish. Smokey had been Grandma's cat but now she was ours, and we all doted on her. She was a saggy old grey cat with rather tired looking fur, but she still liked to sit on top of the wall if the sun was shining. Grandma had adored her.

"Do you remember how she always slept on Gran's bed?" said Barbara as we watched Smokey eagerly awaiting her milk. I nodded. Mum wouldn't let the cat up on our beds, saying it was unhealthy.

Ba sat down at the table and pulled the thick catalogue towards her and turned to the fashion pages. I knew Mum only used the catalogue to get cheap household stuff like towels and cheap sheets.

She made most of our clothes herself.

"Cripes, look at that!" Barbara stabbed the picture of a low cut dress in brilliant red. "Reckon I'd look good in that?"

I shrugged. She turned to the jewellery page and passed a hand over some dangly earrings. I sat down next to her and Smokey jumped onto my knee.

"Look Smokes, wouldn't they suit me?"

A Frankie Vaughan tune sounded. It meant the end of Mick's lesson. Dad always let him end with some pop stuff. I got up and hung about the door waiting for him to come out.

"Where's the bonfire going to be this year?" I asked him. It was always in the back street somewhere, and last November 5th it was outside our house. Dad had stayed indoors, of course, scared of the noise and fire. It seems awful to me that Dad was so brave in the war and now suffers from the after effects of his accident when he hears loud noises. Mum said she didn't want the bonfire here again. It blistered all the paintwork on the gate, but I thought it was more likely to be because of Dad.

"It's going to be up the top end by the Red Lion pub."

"What? At Beryl's place?" The pub was where she lived.

"Yes."

"Be good if it was in the pub yard wouldn't it?"

"Great." He tucked his music under his arm.

Ba buried her head in the catalogue again, but I knew she was ear-wigging. She used to love Bonfire Night. Once she said it was the best night in the year.

"Barbara, do you want to come and play a duet with me?" It was Dad calling.

"Sorry Dad too busy. Homework and all that." She slammed the book shut and scampered upstairs.

Then as soon as Mick had left she came creeping down the stairs in a tight skirt and skinny rib jumper. With a wink at me and her finger to her lips she quietly opened the door and stole out. And it wasn't for just a minute. She was a long time.

We'd finished tea when Barbara turned up. She looked at me. I knew the look. It meant don't you dare say anything. She'd got her hair loose, instead of it being tied back but she was in her school uniform again.

"Well!" said Mum.

"I went to Bren's to help her perm her hair with one of these 'Twinkie' perms, that are all the rage. They're dead good Mum. They use spin rollers now. I could give you one if you like." Mum took a deep breath.

That evening as we got ready for bed she pushed her hair back. Two gold rings glistened from her ears. She'd had her ears pierced!

"Gosh! Where did you go for that?" You had to be older to get it done in a shop.

"Brenda and me did each other's with a needle and cork," she said. She lay down in bed on her side, winced and turned onto her back.

"Mum will kill you," I said.

Chapter 3

Barbara's Boyfriend

Saturday morning Barbara stayed in bed. Mum couldn't understand why. I knew why. It was the earrings.

"She's always out these days," said Mum. "I suppose I can't grumble if she's in bed. If she's not at Brenda's doing mad things, it's this boyfriend whom I've never even met. And I'm not sure about this boyfriend."

"She's growing up love," said Dad. "Now is it worth me lighting a fire in the front room this weekend?"

Mum shook her head. They only used the front room if we were all going to be in or on special occasions. Coal was expensive. "No, both girls will be out. We'll make do."

As she spoke there was an almighty gurgle and the pipe from the twin tub washing machine flopped out of the sink and snaked on the ground, squirting water everywhere. Our house was not the place to be.

I hopped over the puddle, and went out to see Beryl. She was polishing the tables in the snug. The room smelled of smoke and there was a pile of dirty ashtrays on the bar top.

"Hi," she called as I poked my head round the door, "I was just coming to call for you." She dumped the duster next to the ashtrays, and grabbed her wind jammer.

"Bye Mum," she called. "I've done the dusting."

We nearly always went down to Pier Head on Saturday mornings. It wasn't the same since the overhead docker's railway had gone two or three years ago, but I still loved the sound of the ships on the Mersey, and the seagulls calling and soaring in the wind.

We walked down Lister Street then cut through Corporation Park, where some lads were playing footie. The sun was out but it was breezy and leaves were swirling around our feet as we crossed the damp grass. Rubbish skittered along the pavements, collecting in the corners of buildings. As we got down to the river front I pulled up my coat collar. It was always chilly here.

"Come on it will be warmer in the town and I want to go to Woollies, and get some stamp hinges." Dad had started my sister and me collecting stamps. The three of us used to sit on the floor in front of the fire soaking used ones off the envelopes. But recently Barbara had lost interest, and Dad said I could have the album. 'Kid's stuff,' she'd said. 'You're welcome to it.' I told Beryl about Ba's boyfriend.

"What's she doing going out with that creep?"

I shrugged.

We caught the bus home. A steaming meat and potato pie stood on the table and Mum had made one of her tasty Yorkshire puddings. It rose up like a balloon in its tin. Barbara was at the table and being pleasant. She even began slicing the pie.

"You have a rest Mum," she said when we'd finished the meal. "You've been busy all morning."

Mum picked up the newspaper, and was quickly engrossed in it. "Says here, more new housing on the wastelands," she announced. "Two tower blocks to be built behind the prefabs over Speke way."

Barbara gave a flurry of little coughs. "I'll be out later than usual tonight Mum."

Mum flicked the paper to one side and looked at Dad. Dad shrugged his shoulders.

"Trev's taking me dancing. I've said he can call for me. That will be O.K. won't it? You've no need to ask him in."

Mum folded the newspaper and stood up.

"Well just you remember you're not to go sitting in those late night coffee bars in town." She poked the newspaper. "There's something right here about a fight breaking out between rival gangs last week."

"Oh no Mum. We'll not do that."

Later that evening, Barbara rustled down the stairs in her royal blue dirndl skirt, and sleeveless spotted blouse. She'd soaked the underskirt in sugar water to make it stiff and full. She was wearing a black elastic belt which pinched in her waist, and shoes with high thin heels.

"You'll break your neck dancing in those," said Mum.

Ba tutted, "Honestly Mum, you're so old fashioned. I can't go in flat shoes."

Her glossy black hair was down covering the earrings and I had to admit she looked great. There was a knock at the door.

"That'll be Trev. I'll go," she said as she made to the door. But Mum was there first. "Do come in," she said politely.

He strode in across the threshold. Dad, who was standing with his back to the fire, warming his backside, nodded and moved away.

"It looks cold out there. Have a warm by the fire lad before you go out again." I could see Mum eyeing Trevor up and down. Greasy forelock hanging down his forehead, and hair spiking onto his collar. There was a strong smell of after shave floating round the room.

"Where are you going dancing?" Mum asked.

"Not sure yet. Maybe the place in town."

I saw Mum's face sag.

"Not that Alf Shutts dive by the cinema Mum," said Barbara. "He wouldn't take me there would you Trev?"

"No way," said Trev, putting his arm round Barbara and pulling her closer. "Only the best for my bird."

I saw Mum's stunned expression. Even Ba looked a little uncomfortable. Trevor took a cigarette from his cigarette case, and hung it between his lips, and they left. I ran up to my bedroom and pulled back the curtain. About half way up the street he paused and lit up, dragged on the cig then offered it to Barbara. She pushed his hand away and laughed. That was one thing, she'd always said she'd never smoke. At least she still felt the same about that.

"Well," I heard Mum say to Dad, "that took us all by surprise."

Then Dad was on the piano in the front room, despite the room being cold, and Mum had turned the radio on. Someone was blathering about the recent invention of the hovercraft and the first photos of the other side of the moon. *Moving On* was the name of the programme. I sniffed. That horrid after shave had wafted up the stairs and was invading my bedroom.

Chapter 4

Juke Box Jury

Mick leapt off the couch and turned up the volume on the television as Lonnie Donnegan skiffled for all he was worth in front of us. 'My old man's a dustman, he wears a…"

"Cripes can't he play?" said Mick. "I'm going to get a washboard and thimble and do that." A honking noise sounded from the television. Mick jumped up, throwing his arms in the air. "Yeah yeah! It's a hit."

Mr Turner poked his head round the door.

"Glory be!" he said. "And you want to be like him. Heaven help me and your Mum." Mick laughed.

I stared keenly at the telly as Lonnie Donnegan bowed, and went off waving his guitar. Would it be Elvis Presley next? I had to watch Cliff Richard smouldering on the screen before Elvis appeared, jumping round the stage with the mike almost in his mouth. "Move it Elvis," I yelled. He threw himself down on his knees.

"Watch hard. He splits his trousers sometimes," said Mick.

I ran up to the screen but it was all blurred.

"Missed it," said Mick. "He split 'em just now." He was grinning all over his face. I threw a cushion at him and he rolled on the floor laughing and clasping it to him. David Jacobs wound up the show, and then it was some boring thing about race riots in America and ones in this country over the last two years.

Mick's mum came in. She wanted to watch the Bob Monkhouse programme. Mr Turner shovelled coal onto the fire, which made it crackle and spit then they drew the two easy chairs nearer the fire, and Mick and I sat on the settee.

"Have some toffee Ann." She passed over a baking tin piled with sticky chewy lumps. "I've been practising for November 5th."

She sat back in the armchair, picked up her knitting, and chatted throughout Bob Monkhouse's jokes. It was cosy and friendly, and I wished our house was like that. It used to be until Barbara got difficult and Mum got cross. I didn't want to go home at the end of the programme. But I had to.

I woke up as Barbara crept into our bedroom. Mum had stayed up waiting for her, and I could tell there'd been words. She'd had a great time she said, flopping onto the bed. They'd been to New Brighton's Tower Ballroom, not some grot place in Liverpool.

"**And** we're going to Blackpool sometime – the Tower Ballroom no less. And Trev's getting tickets for the Empire Theatre next week where the 'TV Star Search' is on. He reckons I could well be on television when the cameras flash round the audience. Says I'm pretty enough to be picked out. That group The Quarry Men will be there."

"You mean Johnny and the Moon Dogs. They've changed their names."

She stared at me. "Fancy you knowing about them."

I smiled, one up to me. I snuggled under the candlewick bedspread, as it was getting cold at nights now. Mum had just put us each an extra blanket on the bed.

"The bonfire's going to be up the top of the street this year," I ventured.

"Huh! Treacle toffee and sparklers, and Dad hiding away from the bangers. You can keep it." She sighed and turned over away from me.

"He was better last year," I said. "Besides if

you'd been shot down in a 'plane like he was, bangs and fires might startle you. You've always liked bonfires."

"Yeah well..." She tossed about in bed again and ended up on her back. I could see the shape of her knees push up the bed clothes in the dark.

"Please yourself. We're going to make a guy."

"Well make one of Miss Crag," she replied. We both giggled.

Life wasn't any better in our house the next week. A letter came from the headmistress. Mum read it, and I watched her cheeks go crimson. She took a deep breath, made Barbara sit down at the table. She sent me out of the room, but I listened at the door.

"Being cheeky to Miss Crag. Not wearing your school uniform properly, and what's this, kissing in broad daylight. Her work has plummeted and unless she puts in more effort I see no point in her taking a valuable Grammar School place. Well my girl!"

"Not true." Barbara's voice was defiant. "Miserable cows they are at that school. They just stuff you with homework. Even the prefects are horrible. I might leave." I bit my lip. I liked school.

I liked most of our teachers.

"You can stop that silly talk and write a letter apologising." No answer.

"And if you don't, . . ." Mum's voice was loud and clear, ". . . I will."

I rushed upstairs before the door opened and one or other of them stormed out, and into me. Why had she to go and spoil things? I'd always liked my sister despite her bossiness. She came thumping up the stairs and carried on all the way to the Heights of Abraham, as we called the bathroom in the attic.

I disappeared up to Beryl's. After all it was half term and maybe we could go out and do something. I knew the lads were out in the street chumping (looking for wood for the bonfire). We could do that.

"I've got to stay in and wait for a delivery of crisps and stuff," she moaned. "Mum's out at a 'ban the bomb meeting'. She's worse than ever since she went on that Aldermaston march last year. Doesn't seem to care about anything else. She gave me these for the guy." She tipped a load of clothes out of a bag. I picked up a long skirt and wrapped it round myself.

"It will have to be a girl guy then!" I laughed.

"Mick said the fire's going to be up this end this year. Why don't you ask your dad if we can have it here in the pub yard?"

"Yes, it would be smashing but he's so short staffed."

"He could ask some of the dads to help out? My dad might."

She looked at me. "Your dad?" She knew about his problem.

"Well not outside with the fire, but here in the bar he'd be O.K."

"Right. I'll ask him again. I'll pick a good moment and suggest it."

I left to go back home and had just turned the corner when BANG! An enormous crack like a gun shot sounded.

I stopped. Dad was lurching round the corner, he looked haggard and fearful and as though he was crying. Only he wasn't crying. He was shaking and upset. He gasped as he saw me. "Can't even get fish and chips without this happening," he mumbled. He was trembling, fiddling with the fish and chips paper, and I saw he'd spilled most of the chips on the pavement. "It was only a lorry backfiring on the main road," he said. "Will I ever get over this silly carry on of mine?"

I took his arm. "It was sudden though," I said. "It frightened me."

"Are you all right Mr Baker?" Beryl had come out.

"He's O.K.," I said, and we hurried on.

There were kids in the street flicking brightly coloured bottle tops. Some of them saw me holding his arm. I could see the lad who'd called him a nutcase once. Fortunately the coal cart moved into the middle of the road, blocking their view and the coal man took a sack of coal on his shoulder ready to lower it into number twenty seven's coal hole.

"Hello," he called cheerily to my dad. "Not a bad day is it?"

"No," said Dad, and after that he seemed to calm down.

"You're getting better," I told him.

He smiled. "Reckon? Yes I'll beat it in the end I suppose."

Chapter 5

Fireworks

"See what I've got from the shop!" Mum laid two brown paper bags on the table. Six long sparklers protruded from one of them and I quickly opened the other.

"Wow Mum!"

"Mr Jones let me have a discount, so you've got a 10 shilling box this year." Pictures of coloured fireworks almost fizzed off the lid - exploding rockets, whirling pinwheels, and falling stars.

"Gosh, thanks Mum." I opened the box and took a deep sniff. I loved the exciting smell of the gunpowder tinged with danger. I plucked the snuggling fireworks from their thin blue paper and stood them in a row. Tall Roman candles first, then the cones - Snowflake and Vesuvius, the white pinwheel and lastly the brown coiled jumping crackers. I was always wary of those. Lads like Tony Bullock used to sneak up and light one behind you. Barbara was looking over my shoulder at the fireworks. She'd always liked fireworks, and was braver about the bangs than I was. I put them all back in the box, took my coat off its hook and slung it round my shoulder. "Going round to show them to Mick, Mum."

"O.K. love."

"May go up to Beryl's too."

As I opened the door I saw both Beryl and Mick playing out in the street with the other kids. They all came running over to me.

"Guess what! Beryl's dad says we can have the fire in the pub yard.

"Yeah!" Mick pinged a stone at the lamppost, making a hollow sound. "Brilliant!"

"Oh great!" I gave the thumbs up sign to Beryl, who responded by telling everyone it had been my idea. And then I remembered my offer of Dad helping in the bar. How could I have done that, and without even asking him first. He wouldn't want to help out at a really big bonfire, even if he was inside the pub, not with all those bangs. He might even have another of his turns. My stomach began to churn with the thought.

"Some of your dads will have to help though. Mine can't do everything on his own," said Beryl. I looked at her and knew she'd twigged what I was thinking. "Then your dad won't have to come," she whispered. A few kids sniggered.

"Yeah don't want him going bonkers," said

one boy. I marched up and grabbed his coat collar.

"It's called Trauma," I said, "from the war, when he was very brave, so there." I tugged hard on his collar.

"Oh softy that was years ago."

"So!" I said. I'd had enough. I wanted to be back home by my nice quiet dad. "I'm going."

I walked back down the street, my footsteps echoing.

I could hear Beryl's footsteps catching up with me.

"I didn't mean to start anything. We are still friends aren't we?" I bit my lip and nodded, then hurried home.

Barbara was in for once. She was toasting her bare feet by the fire, resting her glossy red toe nails on the fender.

"You'll get chilblains" Mum was saying. Barbara tutted and moved them off the fender. Mum turned to me. "You'd better put those fireworks somewhere safe love."

"I'll put them in the shed, shall I?"

"Yes, that's a good idea. Lock the door." I did as she said then came back, and plonked myself on the hearth rug in front of Mum's legs.

"The coals a bit damp," said Dad. "It won't burn up properly, not like the good old stuff my mother used to get. Remember her fires."

"Roaring ones," said Barbara. She drew up her knees and tucked her arms around them. "She used to grade coal didn't she, when she worked?"

Dad nodded. "Yes, hard, dirty work."

I couldn't believe it. Barbara was actually talking to us, joining in about Grandma. We were being like a normal family again. But then she had always loved Dad's mother.

"Smokey used to sit on my knee whilst Grandma brushed my hair, or sometimes cooked toast in front of the fire on that pronged toasting fork of hers." She reached out to Smokey, who was curled up in front of the fire. But the cat just walked off, and Barbara looked disappointed. "She never comes to me now."

"She's getting too hot, near the fire," said Mum.

"Her hands were lined black," said Barbara,

"Grandma I mean, not Smokey."

We laughed.

"Well she had the allotment," said Dad, "there was always soil or coal dust on her hands."

"Yes and look what's happened to it," said Barbara.

Dad looked uncomfortable. "I've not had time to do much to it."

"You picked the runner beans," said Mum, but we all knew that was all he'd done, and none of us had helped.

"You've just let it go," said Barbara, her voice suddenly taking on its usual tone, "like you do everything, everything except your bloomin' piano stuff. You owe it to Gran to do something."

Mum turned sharply to face her. "And you owe your father a bit of respect young lady."

Barbara flicked back her long hair and the gold rings flashed in the firelight. Mum was out of the leather armchair. "Are those earrings in your ears my girl?"

"And what if they are? Haven't you seen

earrings before?"

"Common!" said Mum. "That's what you're turning out to be."

"Grandma had pierced ears," said Barbara, "and no one called her common."

Dad got up. He said nothing. He turned on the light. The cosy magical shadows disappeared. Everything was bright and clear and ugly. Barbara left the room and went upstairs. She didn't thump about but went quietly, almost silently. Somehow that seemed worse. I didn't understand her at all these days, but she wasn't happy.

Chapter 6

Trouble in the Fog

Beryl and I made a lady guy with the old clothes.

The lads in the street jeered at it. "Ooh la la, come with me Baby."

We laughed, called her Millie and left her standing against the pub wall.

"Come on let's go make a real proper guy," they said and slumped off to make the usual raggy scruffy thing they always produced.

"Mum's left me a list of shopping to do in town," said Beryl "but it won't take long, and she says I can spend the change. How about us going up to that new Wimpy Bar for a beef burger?"

I'd never been in a Wimpy bar, or had a beef burger before, but it was great. Beryl picked up her burger and wrapped the bottom half in a serviette.

"This is how you eat them," she mumbled, taking a huge bite out of the roll. "Mmm! Scrumptious."

A piece of onion dangled from her mouth. I laughed as she folded it back into her mouth and squirted tomato sauce into my burger.

"Mmm!"

"It's a new idea from America," she said. "You've got ketchup on your chin."

We left the Wimpy and walked along the main road. I gazed up at a tall office block being built. It was all concrete and glass.

"Have you seen those skyscraper blocks of flats up Abbey Road?" said Beryl. "They nearly reach the sky. Dad says we'll be like New York if this goes on."

I was looking at the sky reflected in all the windows in the block, dull grey, not blue with puffy peach clouds which they might be in Summer. It was coming in dark early, and there was a mist. I wrapped my arms around myself. A dampness had crept in from the sea. There was an eerie glow around us. And then came the blast of a foghorn from the Mersey. FOG! I could see it now, flowing in fast! We hurried. So did the fog, swirling round our chilling legs. The traffic slowed, and their sounds seemed muted. I took Beryl's hand.

Very soon we found ourselves in a knot of people.

"We're outside one of the clubs where the pop groups practise," said Beryl.

All I could see were heads and shoulders pushing and shoving in the scrap of light from the doorway. We tried to force our way through, but the crowd swelled more and more. A policeman's torchlight skimmed over our heads and along the faces.

"Barbara," I cried, "there's Barbara," but the torch passed on and a policeman shoved past me.

"Mind out love." He was dragging a fellow.

"It's not my fault. He was trying to chat up my girl," the struggling lad was yelling now. "Let me go."

Another lad followed him, wiping blood from his face. "Don't kid yourself Ryan. Anyway what if I did?"

It was Trevor.

Then I heard Barbara's pathetic cry.

"Trev!"

She was near enough for me to touch if only I could worm through the waving arms. She grabbed Trevor's jacket tails, but he shook her off.

"Leave me be will you." He lurched off into

the fog and left her there in the dispersing crowd. I rushed up to her. She was crying. I swear it. She wiped her hand across her cheeks.

"You're better off without him Love," someone called. I took her arm. But when we got to the bus stop her face was dry.

"It were nothing," she said, "just a bit of a scrabble. Trev wouldn't look at another woman. He loves me."

"Well he's left you to find your own way home in this fog."

She was quiet then said, "Don't tell Mum will you?"

We waited ages for a bus and eventually one came. Whatever the fogs were like the buses rarely let us down.

Chapter 7

Enough of Barbara

By Sunday evening nearly every shed or yard in the street was stuffed with wood, ready for the bonfire. Dads from the street had volunteered to help Beryl's father. Beryl said he was real chuffed by all the support. Our street was a friendly street and we were good at helping one another. It was back to school tomorrow.

"**I've** replied to your headteacher young lady, as you haven't," said Mum as she held out a letter to Ba. "Either you give it in or I post it."

Ba reached out her hand. "I'll take it."

Mum held on to the letter. "Now promise me you will hand it in Barbara." Barbara nodded. "I said promise."

"Promise," she said sulkily. "Cross my heart and hope to die."

Mum let her take the letter, which she put in her pocket.

We sat together on the bus. Ba tried to open the letter but realised she couldn't without damaging the envelope. She sighed and began saying how she would enjoy Christmas, now she had a boyfriend. I couldn't believe her, not after what had happened.

"But Ba he let you down."

"Don't start Ann. It's nothing to do with you." She paused. "Anyway I've always liked Christmas."

"Remember how we went carol singing with the church choir last year?" I said.

"It was O.K." She turned to look out of the window. "The best Christmases were when Grandma was alive and we went round to her house." I remembered how Dad used to play the piano after the sherries and mince pies.

"We always ended up singing, all of us," said Barbara. "I liked that."

"And you'd show off by singing on your own," I said.

We got off the bus and walked across town for the next bus. "See you after school." I said.

"Yeah but don't wait about."

"You're not going to see that Trevor are you?"

I shouldn't have said anything. We'd been getting on well.

"What if I am?"

"You're mad that's what!"

"Don't you call me mad."

"And stupid and barmy."

She flung her satchel round by its strap so that it caught me on the shin. It hurt but I was too mad to let her see that.

"Right!" I flung my packed lunch at her.

The lid burst open and I watched my sandwiches fall out into the gutter as she ran off laughing. I kicked them down the drain, and made my way to school. When I got there I noticed my leg. The buckle on her satchel had scratched it and there was a thin red line of blood all the way to my ankle sock, where it had soaked in.

The day dragged. The weather was dull and boring, greyness everywhere. I was glad when it was time to go home.

I gazed idly at the adverts as they skimmed past the bus. I don't know why they interested me

so much but they did. At the Bankfoot stop the Oxydol poster on the front of the bank was just about level with my eyes. It was a vivid orange spiral. I was in a spiral, pulled into something I didn't want to be in. I wondered if Barbara had handed in Mum's letter. And if so, would it be all right? And if not, what then?

Chapter 8

The Scare of Our Lives

It was almost dark when I got home. The back street was full of shadows but the houses looked warm and friendly with their lights on. Dad was sitting on the piano stool holding a pencil in his teeth and rubbing out some notes on a piece of sheet of music.

"I thought Mick could play this with me when he comes round."

"Shall I sing to it?" I offered. We both laughed, knowing my singing voice sounded like Smokey's squeaky toy.

The kitchen door opened and Barbara put her head round the door.

"Hello Dad." She didn't say anything to me. I was glad. I didn't want to speak to her anyway. I didn't even look at her. She came in and dumped her schoolbag down the side of the piano.

"No homework tonight," she said.

"Are you sure?" said Dad, trying out his new notes on the keys.

She went back to the kitchen and turned on the radio. They were talking about this new big wide road they were building. Part of it beginning at St. Albans was already open. It was to run North to South through the country. It had three lanes. It sounded dead dangerous to me. I wondered what they'd invent next. Things were altering, moving on as Mum would say. New buildings were going up everywhere, there seemed to be more food and goods in the shops, and people were travelling abroad for holidays on huge 'planes called jets. We didn't, but Ba said she knew lots of folk who did. I could see her putting lipstick on through the reflection in the mirror. She twisted the rings in her ears, pulling a face. I went back into the kitchen.

"You have to keep the holes open. It takes six weeks. Trev can't wait for me to wear danglies. Says I've got to wear the ones he bought me."

"Put your head in a bucket if he told you to, would you?" I sneered.

Smokey came purring and winding between our legs. Barbara bent down to stroke her. "You're the only one in this house who doesn't go on at me," she said. The cat swished its tail and went on its way.

"Oh diddums," I snapped. She lashed out at me, but I dodged, and Mum's favourite jug came flying off the shelf and crashed into pieces.

"Whatever's going on?" called Dad. Neither of us answered and he didn't come to see.

"I'm sick of this house," said Barbara frantically sweeping up the bits and shovelling them into the bin. "Thank goodness I'm going out with Trev tonight."

"Where are you going?"

"Wouldn't you like to know," she replied, then stormed upstairs.

Mum cooked us bacon and eggs when she came in. Neither of us told her about the broken jug.

"I'm going to the Roxy with Flo to see that new Albert Finney film," she said, dishing out the sausages. "First show, so I'd better get a move on. It starts at six thirty."

"You're always out, either at work or the flicks. Hardly any of my friends' mums work," said Ba.

Mum slammed a plate down in front of her, but said nothing.

Barbara seemed on edge after Mum had gone.

She kept pulling the curtain aside and peering out. She'd put her coat on ready and kept fiddling with something in her pocket, as though to make sure it was still there.

"He's coming to meet me," she said. Then suddenly she dashed to the door. "He's here." She swung her new red scarf round her neck. "Bye Dad."

"Bye love."

I started straight away on making my turnip lantern. I made one every year for bonfire night. It was hard work scraping out the inside, and every year I vowed I'd not make another but I always did. The wall gas fire glowed a cosy orange, and I began listening to 'Have a Go Jo' on the radio. I heard the whine of a rocket climbing into the sky, and pulled back the curtains to watch it explode. Out fell the bright green stars, turning the sky around green. It was dazzling! I blinked trying to get my eyes in focus again and looked down the yard. I gasped. There was a light coming from the shed window, a cigarette light. Someone was in there. I opened the kitchen door. Voices! Raised voices, Ba's and Trev's. And then as I went outside there was an enormous BANG - a bang I shall not forget as long as I live.

"DAD!" I yelled and sped down the path.

Chapter 9

Rescue

The door flung open and Trevor burst out. He leapt up the steps from the shed, dropping his cigarette on the floor, and ran up the yard.

"BA!" Dad was beside me. Bangs! More bangs! Crack! The window blew out, and flames from the wood leapt up. Dad was in the shed. Barbara was screaming. She was cowering with one arm in front of her eyes. He grabbed her arm and pulled. I tried with all my might to shift one of the wooden stakes out of their way. But as she got on her feet pieces of flame-edged wood fell across her ankles. Dad slung them aside with his bare hands.

"Get back Ann." He staggered out, with Barbara in his arms. A tiny flame crept onto the fringe of her scarf. I whipped the scarf from her.

"QUICK TREV HELP!"

I looked up the yard. He'd gone! Mick was climbing over the fence.

"Call the fire brigade," I yelled. "Tetley's house. They're the nearest with a phone."

Barbara was sitting on the bottom door step

shaking. Mick's mum was with her and Dad.

"Let's get you into the house now, Chuck," she said hitching Ba's arm over her shoulder, telling Dad to take the other one. Barbara was crying, but apart from cuts, and dirt she didn't seem badly injured. Dad had blood streaming down his face where the window glass had sliced him, but he just kept wiping it up with the back of his hand. I put the kettle on. I looked at Dad. How had he coped with all these bangs and flames? But he had. He was the one in charge now, without a wobble in sight.

"Really sweet tea," he ordered as I reached for the sugar bowl. He'd already asked Mick's mum to fetch a blanket off the beds upstairs, to wrap round Barbara. "Get the first aid box Ann, and get me a plaster to stick over this cut, to stop the bleeding." I did as he said. Mick was back, hot and sweating.

"They're coming. Everyone's out in the street. Even Barraclough's from down the end." I could hear them, clattering towards our house.

"Don't let 'em come in, we've enough on. Just say she's all right."

"Where's Trev?" Barbara said suddenly.

"Don't worry yourself about him, love." Dad

wrapped the blanket round her shoulders.

"He's GONE," I said with all the disgust I could manage. She looked up at me through her straggling hair.

"The Toad."

"Have a sip of tea, Ba," said Dad.

She wriggled her arms out of the blanket and clasped the mug with two hands.

"Ugh, it's sickly!" It was good to hear the defiance in her voice again.

"Drink it Ba," he urged, looking her firmly in the eyes. She did, every last drop.

The fire engine rang its way up the narrow street. Mick's mum shot out to meet it. There wasn't much wood left in the shed, only a few planks. Tongues of flames were licking the stonework in vain and the bangs had stopped.

"Anyone injured? Do we need an ambulance?" The firemen jumped down.

"No, no," shrieked Barbara. "I'm not going to hospital."

"I think we're best left quiet," said Dad. And then I saw the cut on his cheek. Blood was pouring from the cut under the sodden red plaster.

"Dad, your cheek,"

"It's nothing. I'll see to it in a moment."

It took only minutes to put out the fire. It hadn't been a big fire but it had seemed tremendously threatening in there. All the kids in the street got a strict warning about behaving themselves and not being silly with fireworks. Of course it wasn't their faults. It was mine. They were my fireworks. What if Ba or Dad had died in there, or they'd been really badly burned? My heart creased in half with thoughts of what might have been.

"I'm going to have a bath," said Barbara, after things had calmed down.

"Not after the shock you've had," said Dad. "It's too cold in the bathroom."

"Come on, I'll help you get washed in the sink like we used to before we had the bathroom," I said.

As Barbara was getting into her woollen dressing gown Mum burst in. She took one look at us all. "What's up?"

Barbara turned to her and threw her arms around her, then started crying into Mum's shoulder. "Tell me Ba. What's happened?" She saw Dad's face. "Bill!" We told her about the fire.

"But…"

"It's my fault," I said. "I must have left the key in the door." Barbara pushed herself out of Mum's arms.

"It's not your fault. I took the key. Trev wanted me to get the fireworks down from the shelf for this party thing with his mates. Then he lit a cig. I told him to put it out. He wouldn't. He just laughed. There wasn't room I told him. Then he moved towards the window, fell over the wooden stakes, grabbed the shelf and the fireworks came off." Her voice was rising. She began crying again. "Honest Mum I tried to make him give up. I'm sorry. Sorry."

"Hush Ba." Mum was stroking her hair like Grandma used to do. Ba dragged me into the hug.

"Is someone going to take a look at this cut on my face?" said Dad. Mum rushed to him and peeled back the thick wedge of cotton wool he had stuck there.

"It needs stitching," she said.

"Not tonight," said Dad.

"Well first thing in the morning."

We all drank cocoa together and, despite everything, there was a warmness in my heart which had been missing for weeks. There came a tiny 'meow'. It was Smokey. She'd been hiding upstairs.

"Oh Smokey," said Barbara. And do you know what? That cat seemed to understand her. She went and sniffed all round Barbara's feet then at her dressing gown, and finally she leapt up onto Barbara's knee and settled down. I saw another tear slide from the corner of Barbara's eye. I bit my lip. Poor old Barbara. She'd had a rotten time. But perhaps things would be better now.

Chapter 10

Moving on

November the fifth dawned with the weak sun polishing our cobbled back street. We were going to school together again, Ba and me. She'd not seen Trevor since the fire, or even mentioned his name.

We were on the bus home.

"You *are* coming to the bonfire tonight aren't you?" I asked, as I watched a cluster of pink stars cascade down the back of the new supermarket.

"'Course I am," she said, as though it was something I should never have doubted. "Even Old Cragface has let us off homework." She followed my gaze. "That supermarket's open at last."

"Yes." Its windows were plastered with star shaped stickers promising price cuts. It was the first one near us. Dad reckoned supermarkets would spring up all over the place in the next few years, like the Chinese restaurants were doing. "The sixties will be full of them, getting larger and larger all the time," he'd said. Mum said it would start the decline of shopping as we knew it, and kill the small corner shops.

"I like supermarkets," said Ba. "No queuing

like at the co-op. And their meat counters are much better than smelly butcher's shops with sides of cows and rabbits hanging from the wall, and manky sawdust everywhere."

Ba was fond of animals and had always been upset by butchers' shops.

"Look!" Another rocket zoomed up, leaving a golden trail. The bus slowed down and stopped.

We heard the lads getting on at the Bankfoot stop, and Tony Bullock's loud bragging voice telling them how his brother had escaped from a huge fire in our shed, after saving my sister's life. Ba sprang up like a Jack in a box and pushed past me. She strode to the top of the stairs, stretched her arms, and barred his way.

"Is that what he told you all?" she called out. "Lies, lies, all of it. He ran away and left me, that's what!"

Tony looked up, his cheeks crimson. "Shift yourself Grub," he said. She stood firm.

He tried to head-butt her but was too near for it to have any effect. The kids below began jeering.

"Frightened of a lass are you Tony?" He was trapped. Ba dropped down a step forcing him down too, and causing a commotion on the stairs.

"Stop fooling about up there," shouted the conductor.

They didn't stop, so he turned the lads off. Ba bounced back into her seat beside me, a big grin on her face. We heard them all yelling at Tony Bullock on the pavement. We looked out of the window. One lad was clouting him with his schoolbag, others were pummelling his back as he crouched with his arms on his head.

"Brilliant Ba," I said.

"Yes kiddo. Great wasn't it?"

The air was laced with the smell of early bonfires as we got off the bus. Big bangs and faint ones shot into the darkness. The magic had begun. We approached the top of our street, turned the corner and there was the pub; lighting up the pub yard was the tall bonfire standing in the middle of it.

"Golly! Is that where it's going to be?" Ba had been completely out of touch with bonfire plans and didn't know it was at the pub.

Dad popped his head out.

"DAD!"

He grinned. "Surprised eh? Your mum's come home early. She's doing beans on toast, then you can both come back and help."

We ran home, hurried down our tea, then scrambled into old trousers as we did every bonfire night.

Beryl was stirring soup. The street lads were milling round giving shrill piercing whistles and bossing one another, as ever. Dad was getting the hang of using the beer pumps while Beryl's mum was washing enough forks for a football crowd.

"One day someone may think to invent a dishwasher we can all afford," she said as I picked up the tea towel.

The light from the pub was casting shadows across the rough stony ground. Our guy, Millie, who was still leaning by the wall cast a really long one. I saw Beryl had pinned a note on her hand.

'Welcome to our bonfire party' it said. I laughed.

"That's great," I said as Beryl and her dad began moving benches. "I'm glad she's not going on the fire."

And then it all began.

The lads dragged their guy, fat as a barrel, and dressed in a plastic mac, towards the bonfire, and with a bit of help from the dads, hoisted it on top. Then with great ceremony Mick's dad set light to the fire. The base glimmered and flickered. Another taper went into it and flames sprang up from the newspaper base, crackled and glowed, and that was it. Our bonfire was going. Everyone cheered. Dad, standing in the doorway, winked at me.

Fireworks whizzed and banged, spurted and died, flashed and exploded. The usual fluttering in my stomach wasn't there this year. Dad came and stood beside me. I felt safer somehow with him around.

The women were coming up the street carrying trays of toffee, potatoes to bake in the fire, and gingerbread. And they stayed. Beryl's mum came out.

"There's pie and mushy peas," she said and people surged into the pub and came out carrying steaming platefuls of food.

The fire was gradually dying down now, and the fireworks were spent. Us kids were stuffing the last blackened baked potatoes into our mouths, and the men were drinking beer.

"Give us a tune Bill," someone said. I saw

Beryl's dad slap mine on the shoulder.

"Yes go on mate," and Dad, who didn't need much persuading after his pint, sat at the pub piano and played.

"Summat we know," called Mick's mum, and soon all the adults were singing, and we kids were joining in. I glanced at Ba, her face smiling and rosy in the firelight. Then in a patch of quietness she suddenly stood up on one of the benches and began singing. There was immediate silence as her smooth clear voice cut through the air. She certainly was a beautiful singer. I smiled. She was over Trev, back to her old self and her music. Everyone clapped and clapped, which made us feel wonderfully proud.

The crowd began thanking Beryl's parents for a lovely evening. One man doffed his cap at Millie and thanked her too!

None of us spoke as we opened the gate by our singed shed. Barbara fumbled in her pocket. "I'm going to rejoin the school choir," she said. She handed an envelope to Mum.

"The note Mum. I never did give it in." Mum, tutted and shook her head. Then she laughed and tore it into tiny pieces.

"I think we've moved on from that," she said,

"all of us." She put her arm round Barbara. I rushed upstairs and took Smokey from the airing cupboard where Mum had made her a nest so she wouldn't hear the bangs much. I brought her down in my arms, and put her down by her cat dish. But the funny thing was, she didn't touch her food but began purring. Then she wove her way round and round our legs, as though she too, was glad things had moved on.

Educational Printing Services Limited
publish a full range of teachers' resources,
pupils booklets and paperbacks.

Order on-line @
www.eprint.co.uk